Suddenly there was a loud hiss. A moment later, a sleek black cat jumped down from a garden wall. She landed in front of them. Her green eyes gleamed as she looked hungrily at Clover. Her long tail lashed from side to side.

"Help!" Clover gasped.

More Best Friends follow soon!

Best Friends

Carrot and Clover

by Jenny Dale

Illustrated by Susan Hellard

A Working Partners Book

MACMILLAN CHILDREN'S BOOKS

To everyone at Freshbrook First School

Special thanks to Liss Norton

First published 2002 by Macmillan Children's Books
a division of Macmillan Publishers Limited
20 New Wharf Road, London N1 9RR
Basingstoke and Oxford
www.panmacmillan.com

Associated companies throughout the world

Created by Working Partners Limited
London W6 0QT

ISBN 0 330 39856 3

3 5 7 9 8 6 4

A CIP catalogue record for this book is available from
the British Library.

Typeset by SX Composing DTP, Rayleigh, Essex
Printed and bound in Great Britain by Mackays of Chatham plc, Kent

chapter one

"I've found a hole!" cheeped Clover. The little yellow chick had been looking for a way to explore the rest of the garden for ages. A tiny corner of the wire netting around her run was loose. If she could just pull the wire aside, it might make a hole big enough to let her squeeze through.

Clover pushed the wire netting with her beak. The hole got a bit bigger. She chirped with excitement. Soon, she would be able to explore the rest of the garden!

Clover's friend Carrot lazily opened one eye to see what Clover was up to. The bunny had been fast asleep in his hutch, which was next to the henhouse. He had been dreaming about juicy carrots. But Clover had cheeped so loudly it had woken him up!

"Clover, what's wrong?" he snuffled. Still half-asleep, he hopped outside to see what was going on. He looked round the run and spotted Clover by the wire netting. It looked as though she was stuck! Carrot hopped over to the fence. "Are you all right?" he asked.

"Of course I am," Clover cheeped. "I'm going to explore!"

Carrot waggled his long ears. He didn't like the sound of that. "We're not allowed out on our own," he snuffled.

"I just want to have a look round," Clover cheeped. She tugged at the wire netting again to make the hole big enough for Carrot. "Come with me!" she begged, as she wriggled through into the garden.

Carrot wasn't sure. Clover was always getting into trouble! Before he could say

anything, the back door of the house opened. Their owner Lucy came out, holding her toast in her hand.

"Look out, Clover!" squeaked Carrot. Usually he loved seeing Lucy. She brought yummy things to eat and she spent ages stroking his ears. But he didn't want Clover to get into trouble for being outside.

"Uh-oh!" Clover chirped. She didn't want Lucy to find out about the hole either. She might block it up.

"Come back inside," Carrot called. He hopped over to the gate to wait for Lucy.

Clover tried to get back in, but the wire netting had flapped back over the hole. She pushed it as hard as she could, but it wouldn't move.

Carrot looked round, expecting to see Clover behind him. But she still wasn't there. He had to stop Lucy seeing what Clover was up to! He jumped on to Lucy's shoe as she came through the gate.

"Morning, Carrot," said Lucy, with her mouth full of toast. She shut the gate, then bent down and stroked his soft, silvery fur.

Carrot rolled over so that Lucy could rub his tummy. He watched Clover out of the corner of his eye, and saw her squeeze through the gap at last.

Clover rushed over to Lucy and Carrot. "Phew!" she cheeped breathlessly. She jumped up on to Lucy's hand.

Lucy stroked Clover's fluffy yellow
feathers with one finger. "Hello, Clover,"
she said. "I wondered where you were."

"I think you should stay in the run
from now on," Carrot squeaked.

"Not likely!" Clover chirped. "I'm
going exploring later." She pecked some
toast crumbs off Lucy's fingers.

Lucy took a carrot out of her pocket

and laid it on the grass. "A carrot for Carrot!" she said.

"My favourite!" Carrot squeaked. He took a big, crunchy bite.

Mrs Green, Lucy's mum, opened the back door. "Hurry up, Lucy," she called. "Or you'll be late."

"Coming, Mum!" Lucy called back.

Lucy stroked Carrot's ears. "I can't be late for school," she told Carrot and Clover. "We're having a Spring Festival today."

Carrot licked some crumbs off Lucy's lap while he was listening. They were very tasty!

"We've been making things for the festival all week," Lucy went on. "There will be lots of chicks and bunnies there."

Clover looked up. Chicks and bunnies!

"Lucy!" Mrs Green called again.

"Goodbye, you two," Lucy said smiling. "I'll see you after school." Still munching her toast, she ran off up the garden with her ponytail swinging behind her.

"School sounds like fun," Clover chirped.

"Yes," snuffled Carrot. "I wonder what Lucy and her friends do there?" He nibbled a bit more of his breakfast carrot.

"And what is a *festival*?" cheeped Clover.

Carrot wrinkled his nose. "I don't know. But it must be good if Lucy likes it."

8

Suddenly Clover jumped up. "*I* know what we can do!" she chirped.

"Oh dear," Carrot squeaked. Most of Clover's ideas led to all sorts of trouble.

Clover flapped her tiny wings madly. "Let's go and find school!"

Chapter Two

"But we're not allowed out of the run," Carrot squeaked.

"Don't you want to find out what school is?" cheeped Clover. She darted over to the hole in the fence and pushed her head through the gap.

"I suppose so," Carrot snuffled. He did feel a bit excited, but there were so many things that could go wrong. "How will we find it?"

"We'll ask someone," Clover chirped. She squeezed through the hole into the garden. "Come on!"

Carrot looked through the netting.
There were some *very* juicy-looking
lettuces in the vegetable patch . . .

"Hurry up," cheeped Clover from the
other side of the wire.

Carrot pushed his nose through the
gap in the fence and sniffed. The grass
smelled lovely. So did the lettuces! He
was much bigger than Clover, so he
would need a bunny-sized hole to
squeeze through. He hooked one paw
through the netting and pulled it back.

Then he flattened his ears and pushed
his whole head through the gap. He put
one paw through, then another. The
wire pressed against his fur. Carrot took
a deep breath and made himself as

small as he could.

One more wriggle, and he was
through! He looked round nervously,
hoping nobody had spotted him.

Clover hopped over to the fish pond in
the middle of the lawn. "The fish might
know the way to school," she chirped.
She peered into the pond. The water
glittered in the sunshine. There were

some orange fish just below the surface.

"Hello," Clover called. The fish didn't move, so she flapped her wings to get their attention.

The fish blew some bubbles.

Carrot hopped over and stared at his reflection in the water. He thought his fur looked very shiny and clean. Then he nibbled a tasty dandelion leaf. He liked the garden, he decided.

Clover leaned forward until her beak was almost touching the water. "Do you know the way to school?" she cheeped.

The fish opened and shut their mouths but only bubbles came out.

"I don't understand bubble-talk," chirped Clover.

The fish blew more bubbles at her.

Then they flicked their tails and dived down in a flash of orange to the bottom of the pond.

"This is trickier than I thought," Clover sighed.

"Never mind," Carrot snuffled. "We can still explore the garden." He scampered across the lawn and tucked into one of the lettuces. They didn't just

smell yummy. They tasted yummy too!

But Clover wanted to keep looking for school. Who else might know the way? Then she spotted a huge black and white creature behind the hedge at the bottom of the garden.

"What's that?" she chirped.

"What's what?" snuffled Carrot, with his mouth full of crunchy lettuce.

"There's something big down there. Look!" Clover cheeped. She ran to the hedge and pushed her way through to the other side. There were lots of these animals, grazing in a big field. They were enormous!

Clover stayed close to the hedge. She didn't want one of them to tread on her by mistake.

Carrot crawled under the hedge to join her. He stared at the creatures in astonishment. He'd never seen such big animals. "What are you?" he squeaked.

One of the animals looked up. "We're cows," she mooed sleepily.

"You don't eat bunnies, do you?" he asked nervously.

"No," the cow replied. "Only grass."

Clover stood up on her tiptoes. "Do you know the way to school?" she cheeped as loudly as she could.

The cow looked puzzled. "Why do you want to go to schooool, little chick?" she asked.

"To find Lucy," Clover chirped bravely.

The cow lowered her huge head

down. She was so close Clover could feel her warm breath ruffling her feathers. "Sorry," the cow mooed. "We don't know the way toooo schooool."

Clover pushed her way back through the hedge sadly. She found a patch of soft grass and sat down to think.

Carrot felt sorry for his friend. She looked fed up. "I'll sit here with you," he

squeaked, snuggling up to her.

Clover nuzzled Carrot's soft fur. She was feeling hot. The sun had moved up the sky and there was hardly any shade in the garden. "It must be lunchtime," she cheeped. "Let's go back into the run and have something to eat."

Carrot yawned and stretched. Then he scratched one ear with his back paw. "Lunchtime?" he snuffled. "That's good. My tummy's rumbling." He hopped towards the run.

Carrot squeezed through the hole. He took a big bite out of a juicy carrot.

Clover hopped through and went to get a drink of water from the bowl. But just then she noticed a trail of toast crumbs in the grass. "Look!" she cheeped.

"These crumbs will show us which way Lucy went. Let's follow them. I want to see those chicks and bunnies!" And off she ran.

Chapter Three

Carrot liked the idea of meeting other chicks and bunnies at school too. But he felt nervous. "Do you think Lucy will be pleased?" he called after Clover.

"Of course she will!" Clover cheeped as she raced across the lawn. She reached the path that led round the side of the house and disappeared.

"Wait for me!" Carrot squeaked. He pushed his way through the hole in the fence and hopped after her.

Clover reached the front gate and

ducked underneath it. She looked along the road. "Bother," she sighed. Lucy had disappeared! Now how would they find their way to school?

Carrot squeezed under the gate and stood on the pavement beside Clover.

"Lucy's gone," cheeped Clover sadly.

Carrot felt secretly relieved. Then he spotted one of the tasty toast crumbs. Yum! Then he found another.

"Oh, well done, Carrot!" Clover cheeped. "You've found a trail."

The line of crumbs went along the pavement and round the corner.

"Lucy went that way!" chirped Clover. She flapped her wings and set off.

Carrot quickly swallowed one more crumb. Then he hopped after Clover.

He was beginning to feel quite excited about being out of the garden.

Suddenly there was a loud roaring noise. A huge metal monster came racing round the corner. It had four wheels and two big, round, shiny eyes.

"Look out!" Carrot squealed. He flattened himself against the pavement.

Clover crouched beside him, staring at the monster in horror. She hoped it didn't eat chicks and bunnies.

The creature roared past without seeing them. "That was close," Carrot squeaked, standing up shakily.

"Very close," Clover agreed. She shook the dust out of her feathers and set off again.

Carrot waggled his ears and followed her.

The trail of crumbs led them along the pavement. Carrot's mouth was watering, but he didn't have time to eat any of them.

Clover went round a corner, then stopped so suddenly that Carrot bumped into her. The trail had stopped. A puppy was licking up the crumbs!

"Oh no!" Clover chirped. "How will we find our way now?"

The puppy looked up. He was white and fluffy with a brown patch over one eye.

He bounded towards them, wagging his tail.

Clover was a little bit frightened. She

stood very close to her friend Carrot.

"Let's play!" the puppy woofed.

"We can't. No time!" Clover cheeped. "We're going to school. Do you know the way?"

"No, I don't. Sorry." The puppy pushed his nose into Carrot's fur and sniffed him.

"Oooh, that tickles!" Carrot giggled.

"Your nose is wet and cold." He pushed the little dog away with his paw.

The puppy licked Carrot's face with his tiny pink tongue.

Carrot shivered and smoothed down his wet fur. Suddenly, he heard a whistle.

"Here, Toby," a man called.

"Can't stop, must go!" barked the puppy. He scampered away towards the man.

Carrot watched as the puppy was led away. "Nice to meet you," he snuffled, rubbing his face with his front paws. Suddenly he noticed that Clover was looking worried. "What's up?" he squeaked.

"The crumb trail's gone," Clover

cheeped. "We need something else to show us the way." She looked along the road. There was a tall post ahead. It had a picture of two children fixed to the top.

Clover stared at it. Maybe it meant that children went this way. Perhaps it meant that school wasn't far! "Look!" she chirped, pointing her wing at the picture. She hopped towards the sign and Carrot scampered beside her.

Suddenly there was a loud hiss. A moment later, a sleek black cat jumped down from a garden wall. She landed in front of them. Her green eyes gleamed as she looked hungrily at Clover. Her long tail lashed from side to side.

"Help!" Clover gasped.

chapter four

"Get behind me!" Carrot squeaked. He wasn't sure what he could do, but he was bigger than Clover and he knew he should try to protect her.

Clover darted behind him. She crouched down so that the cat couldn't see her. Carrot's fur felt warm and comforting.

"Come here, little chickie," the cat hissed.

"Leave us alone!" Carrot growled. He spread his paws and hunched his back, to make himself look bigger.

The cat walked round him. Carrot guessed she was looking for Clover. He turned round at the same time, so that Clover was safely hidden.

"Keep still, big ears!" yowled the cat. She sounded very cross.

Carrot was cross too. He didn't want the cat to hurt Clover. "Leave us alone!"

he grunted again.

Suddenly he sprang forward and struck out with his front paws. The cat leaped back, surprised. She gave an angry howl. Then she turned and ran away with her tail fluffed up.

Carrot stared after her in surprise. He hadn't expected her to run away! He waggled his ears, feeling very pleased with himself.

Clover came out from behind Carrot. "Scaredy cat!" she chirped at the disappearing cat.

"Come on," squeaked Carrot, when the cat was out of sight. "Let's hurry up and get to school."

Soon the pavement got more crowded. There were legs everywhere! But no one seemed to notice Carrot and Clover.

"I didn't think there would be so many people around!" Clover cheeped. She had to keep dodging in and out of the feet. She crouched by the kerb, wondering which way to go. Carrot sat beside her.

A woman and a young girl came along the road. The little girl saw Carrot and Clover. She bent down and stroked them. But her hands were covered with sticky chocolate!

"Yuck!" Clover cheeped, jumping back. She twisted her head round and tried to peck the chocolate out of her feathers.

Carrot's fur was covered in chocolate too, but he didn't mind. "Yummy," he squeaked. He licked the little girl's hand, making her giggle.

The girl's mum hadn't seen Carrot or Clover. She was looking into a shop window a little further down the street. The little girl hurried after her. "Bye-bye, bunny!" she called.

Clover heard the sound of rapid footsteps. She looked round in alarm. A boy was running along the pavement. And he was carrying a bunny *and* a chick! The chick was wearing a bright blue scarf.

"Look, Carrot!" cheeped Clover. She jumped up. "Lucy said there'd be bunnies and chicks at the Spring Festival. That boy must be taking his pets to school."

As the boy came nearer, the bunny

slipped out of his arms. He grabbed it by its ears just before it hit the ground.

"That poor bunny!" Carrot squeaked. He hated being picked up by his ears.

The boy stopped at the edge of the road and looked left and right. There were no metal monsters coming and he hurried across. His bunny and chick looked back at Carrot and Clover with shiny black eyes.

Carrot and Clover scampered across the road after the boy. Clover's legs were starting to ache. She stopped and stretched her toes.

"Don't give up now," Carrot puffed. "I think we're nearly there!"

This side of the road was even more crowded. There were lots of grown-ups walking along. They were talking to each other, so they didn't notice Carrot and Clover.

Clover looked around for the boy with the chick and the bunny. But he had vanished.

Suddenly, Carrot pricked up his ears. "I can hear children," he snuffled.

Clover put her head on one side and listened. She could hear children shouting and laughing. "Me too," she chirped.

Carrot followed the sound along the pavement. It was coming from behind a high wooden fence. Clover hurried after him. The noise grew louder and louder. Carrot felt his ears twitching with excitement.

Suddenly, Carrot reached a wide gap in the fence. On the other side, he could see lots and lots of children running around. One little girl looked very familiar. She was skipping with a group of friends.

"There's Lucy!" Carrot squeaked.

"And there's the boy with the bunny and chick," cheeped Clover, spotting the chick's blue scarf.

A whistle blew. The children began to run into the big building on the other side of the playground.

"Wait, Lucy!" Clover chirped. She ran across the playground. Her legs didn't feel tired any more. They had found school at last!

chapter five

"Come on, Carrot!" cheeped Clover. "Let's look for Lucy." She jumped up some steps and went through an open door into a wide corridor. It was cool and quiet inside. Clover's toes made a tiny scratching sound as she ran along the smooth shiny floor. Carrot's soft paws didn't make any noise at all.

Carrot looked around. There were paintings on the walls high above him. He stretched up so he could see them more clearly. The paintings were of bunnies and chicks. "This is definitely the right place," he snuffled.

Clover reached an open door. She popped her head round and looked into a big, sunny room. There were lots of children sitting at tables, but Lucy wasn't there. Clover couldn't see the chick with

the blue scarf either. "No sign of Lucy yet," she cheeped very quietly to Carrot.

At the end of the corridor they came to an enormous room with a shiny wooden floor and big windows along one side. On the far side of the room was a long table covered with a yellow cloth. Vases of yellow daffodils and red tulips stood on the table. And in between the vases there were lots of bunnies and chicks! One of the chicks was wearing the bright blue scarf.

Clover waved to the chick with her wing. "Hello!" she cheeped. "Are you all right?"

The chick didn't reply.

Carrot scampered up to the table. His pink nose twitched. "I can smell something yummy," he squeaked. "I think I can smell cake!"

There was a chair at one end of the table with a box next to it. Carrot hopped on to the box, then on to the chair, and up on to the table. It was very high. Clover looked like a fluffy yellow dot! Carrot felt dizzy for a moment. He shut his eyes tight, then opened them again. Oh, wow! There were cakes everywhere! Some of them were covered in sticky white icing. And there were plates of little buns dotted with juicy currants.

Carrot sniffed at one of the cakes. The icing stuck to his nose. He licked it off. Yummy!

"Come on, Clover," he said impatiently.

"I can't get up there!" Clover replied.

So Carrot hopped down again and let Clover climb on to his back. Carefully carrying the little chick, he clambered up on to the table.

"Look at the bunnies and chicks!" Clover cheeped excitedly.

Carrot hopped across to a friendly-looking bunny with grey fur. It was wearing a bright yellow ribbon around its neck. "Hello. You look smart," Carrot squeaked.

The bunny didn't say anything.

"I said, *you* look smart!" squeaked Carrot a bit louder. He nudged the bunny with his nose. It fell over.

Carrot jumped back in surprise, straight into the chick with the blue scarf.

The chick wobbled and then fell over too.

Clover ran over to it with a cheep of alarm. "Are you all right?" she asked. "My friend didn't mean to bump into you."

The chick didn't move. Clover touched it with her wing. The chick was very soft, but it didn't feel feathery. She peered closer. "Oh, Carrot. It's not a real chick at all!" she chirped, feeling a bit silly. "It's a toy!"

Then she looked at the bunny with the yellow ribbon. "This bunny's not real either."

Carrot sniffed the other bunnies and chicks. They were *all* toys! Some of them were made from soft felt and some were made out of wool. They had tiny black buttons for eyes and sewn-on mouths. Lucy's classmates must have made them for the Spring Festival, Carrot decided. "Fancy us thinking they were real," he snuffled. He waggled his ears. Then he scampered back to the fruit cake and took another sticky bite.

Suddenly Clover heard a noise like thunder. She stared at the door.

Footsteps! The children were coming!

"Won't Lucy be surprised to see us?" she chirped.

Carrot didn't answer. His mouth was too full of cake. But he twitched his nose to show that he agreed.

Lucy came into the hall. "Lucy!" cheeped Clover. She flapped her wings. Carrot sat up straight and waggled his ears.

But Lucy didn't notice them. She sat down with the other children.

"Let's go over to her," Clover suggested.

More children came into the hall. Carrot looked nervously at the stomping feet. He didn't want to get trodden on. "I think we should wait until everyone's

43

here," he snuffled.

At last the room was full, and all of the children were sitting down.

"Come on," Clover cheeped. But before she could get down, a tall woman came into the hall. Everybody stopped talking and sat still.

"Welcome to our Spring Festival," said the woman.

Clover felt a rush of excitement. Now they were going to find out what the Spring Festival was all about. Suddenly she heard a loud gasp. A boy was looking straight at her!

chapter six

The boy whispered to the children
sitting near him. They all turned round
and stared at Carrot and Clover.

"Hello," Clover cheeped, flapping her
wings at them. More children turned
round.

"Keep still, children," said one of the
grown-ups at the side of the hall.

Clover jumped. The man had a very
loud voice.

"At this time of year, bunnies are born
and chicks hatch out of their eggs," said

the tall woman at the front of the hall.

"*I* hatched out of an egg," Clover chirped proudly to the children sitting next to the table. Several more children looked round.

Carrot nodded. Lucy had been right. The Spring Festival *was* all about chicks and bunnies!

The children began to fidget and whisper to each other. The man with the loud voice stood up. He marched towards the table.

Carrot looked worriedly at the cake next to him. He'd munched a big hole in it! He began to back away. The man looked rather cross. Maybe they were going to get into trouble.

Suddenly Carrot bumped into a cake.

The icing felt very sticky on his fur. He wriggled to get away from it. But the cake slid right off the plate and on to the floor.

"Oh, no!" Carrot squeaked.

The man stepped on the cake. He began to wobble. "Help!" he shouted.

As the man fell, he caught hold of the tablecloth. It jerked and Clover was knocked off her feet. She found herself sliding towards the edge of the table. "Help!" she cheeped, looking round for Carrot.

But Carrot was being dragged off too. He scrabbled at the tablecloth, trying to get a firm hold. But it was no use. He reached the edge of the table and slithered off in a shower of cakes, toys and flowers.

Bump! Carrot hit the floor. He jumped up and looked round for Clover. She was lying next to a toy bunny. "Watch out!" Carrot squealed as a fruit cake splatted on to the floor beside them. Then the tablecloth landed on top of them and everything went very dark.

Carrot popped his head out from under the cloth. "Where are you, Clover?" he squeaked. He had to squeak very loudly because all the children were talking now.

"I'm over here," Clover chirped. She wriggled out from under the tablecloth and shook her wings.

There was a loud groaning noise. Clover froze. Not far away, the man

who'd fallen over climbed to his feet. He
had icing and cake crumbs all over him.
A tiny toy chick was caught on a button
of his shirt. A daffodil was wedged
behind his ear and there was a squashed
bun sticking out of his pocket.

"Are you all right, Mr Jones?" asked a
woman. She helped him to stand up.

"I think so," he said. He brushed some

crumbs off his suit and took the daffodil out from behind his ear. Then he stared at the empty table. "The Spring display is ruined!" he moaned.

Carrot ducked under the tablecloth again. Clover kept very still. She hoped the man would think she was a toy chick. She didn't want to be found now. She had a feeling they might get into a lot of trouble. And she didn't think Lucy would be pleased to see them now.

"I saw two of the toys come to life," a girl said loudly.

Clover held her breath.

"You must have imagined it, Melissa," Mr Jones said.

Melissa shook her head. "No, I didn't. It was a grey bunny and a yellow chick.

They ate one of the cakes."

"Never mind about that now," said Mr Jones. "Let's go back to the classroom." He went out of the room, followed by a line of children. They were whispering to each other and pointing back at the display table.

"Thank goodness they didn't find us," Clover chirped, when everyone had gone.

"Shame we didn't get a chance to sit with Lucy," squeaked Carrot. Now the hall was empty he was feeling much better. "Why don't we have another look for her?"

Clover shook her head. "School's too big for me. Let's go home."

"All right," Carrot agreed. "I'll just have one last bit of cake." He took a big bite out of the fruit cake Mr Jones had trodden on.

"Come on," Clover chirped, scurrying towards the door. Her feet were sore and her wings ached, and she wanted to get home as fast as she could.

"It's good to be back," Clover cheeped later that afternoon. She was snuggled up to Carrot in their run.

Carrot licked a dab of icing from the top of Clover's head. "Do your legs still ache?" he snuffled.

"A bit," chirped Clover. "Are you still feeling sticky?"

"I've licked off most of the icing," he

squeaked. Suddenly he heard the gate rattle. He sat up eagerly. "Lucy's home."

Lucy came round the side of the henhouse. "You'll never guess what happened today!" she said. She sat down on the grass beside them. "Melissa said two toys came to life in the Spring Festival. They ate a cake and knocked everything off the display table."

Clover looked at Carrot. "They don't know it was us, then," she chirped.

"It's such a shame that you couldn't come and see all the chicks and bunnies," Lucy went on. "But I've brought you a piece of fruit cake. It's a bit squashed, but it still tastes nice." She held out the slice of cake on her hand.

"Yummy!" Carrot snuffled, tucking

into a juicy raisin. "Come on, Clover. This is very tasty."

Clover shook her head really hard. "No, thanks," she cheeped. "I've had enough cake for one day!"

Look out for Best~Friends No 1

Snowflake and Sparkle

Snowflake is a puppy with big paws and soft, golden fur. His best friend is Sparkle – a very unusual kitten. She chases balls, scares the postman and begs for treats – just like a dog!

Snowflake longs to be more like Sparkle – but one day, the tiny kitten gets into BIG trouble. Can Snowflake come to the rescue?

Pogo and Pip

Pip the hamster loves his cosy little home. But when his cage door is left open, Pip sees the lovely green garden outside and decides to explore.

The big, wide world is full of danger for a tiny hamster. Soon Pip is running for his life! But a friendly guinea pig called Pogo is watching – will he be able to help?

More Jenny Dale titles!

The prices shown below are correct at the time of going to press. However, Macmillan Publishers reserve the right to show new retail prices on covers which may differ from those previously advertised.

JENNY DALE'S BEST FRIENDS

Snowflake and Sparkle	0 330 39853 9	£3.99
Pogo and Pip	0 330 39854 7	£3.50
Carrot and Clover	0 330 39856 3	£3.50
Bramble and Berry	0 330 39857 1	£3.50
Blossom and Beany	0 330 39775 3	£3.50

JENNY DALE'S PUPPY TALES™

Gus the Greedy Puppy	0 330 37359 5	£2.99
Lily the Lost Puppy	0 330 37360 9	£3.99
Spot the Sporty Puppy	0 330 37361 7	£3.99
Lenny the Lazy Puppy	0 330 37362 5	£3.50

JENNY DALE'S KITTEN TALES™

Star the Snowy Kitten	0 330 37451 6	£3.50
Bob the Bouncy Kitten	0 330 37452 4	£3.99
Nell the Naughty kitten	0 330 37454 0	£3.50

All Pan Macmillan titles can be ordered from our website, www.panmacmillan.com, or from your local bookshop and are also available by post from:

Bookpost, PO Box 29, Douglas, Isle of Man IM99 1BQ
Credit cards accepted. For details:
Telephone: 01624 836000
Fax: 01624 670923
E-mail: bookshop@enterprise.net
www.bookpost.co.uk

Free postage and packing in the United Kingdom